I Love My Mum

'Modern Chinese Masters' is a new imprint of short fiction from contemporary Chinese writers in English translation. Each title has been chosen for its ability to surprise and challenge preconceptions about Chinese fiction.

Cover illustration by Zhang Jie.

Zhang Jie's raw and naked self-portraits remove the artist from her surroundings, placing her in an isolate, empty, solitary world

https://www.zhangjieart.com

I Love My Mum

a novel

by Chen Xiwo

Modern Chinese Masters

Make-Do Publishing,

Hong Kong.

English edition first published 2009.

ISBN 978-988-18419-2-6

Contents

The state's power is absolute: your book can be banned without them needing to provide any reason whatsoever.

Chen Xiwo.

I Love My Mum

Case

1

He stood in front of me. A murder suspect.

I'd just released some prostitutes. They were a bunch of hostesses we'd rounded up from a nightclub. As a crime squad captain, it was my job to keep our streets clean, but I had never foreseen these consequences. There were numerous injured parties: without a sex industry, the entertainment business took a hit; if the entertainment business suffered, that was bad news for hotels; with hotels half empty, fewer people went out at nights, and so the taxi drivers didn't have many customers and roamed like ghosts, slamming their steering wheels and cursing the authorities. The whole city was rebellious: the traffic police couldn't issue any fines; the industry and commerce ministry couldn't

collect any fees; the tax bureau couldn't receive
any taxes. Profits were down, bosses were upset.

My superior, Qian Yi, trembled as he
lectured me. 'The sex industry is a pillar of our
city's economy. Don't you want us to get rich?
Well, a city has to rely on whatever it has. What
we have here is prostitutes. There's no choice but
to release them.'

These prostitutes knew the score. They took
their sweet time getting their things together. One
even put her hairclip in her mouth, and then with
unhurried insolence put up her hair. I suggested
that they should change jobs, and they looked at
me. Those looks were eloquent.

I said, 'So you are only willing to sell your
bodies.'

'Why shouldn't we? Not to sell is a waste.'
They laughed. 'Our bodies are gifts from our
parents. Just like your parents made you one metre
eighty: perfect for making arrests.'

'I don't arrest people because I'm tall.' I looked stern. 'I represent the law. Law needs reasons.'

'When you arrest someone, the reason all depends on you,' they said.

I admit that in this job my size and strength are big assets. My victims, whether or not they are guilty, all look guilty. On my beat, if adults wanted to scare kids they would say: 'I'll call One Metre Eighty to lock you up.'

My nickname, One Metre Eighty, was a wedding gift. My wife's family was comfortably well off, and many men liked her, but she only had eyes for me. At the wedding, when we were playing the traditional wedding games, people asked her why she had chosen me. She laughed but then briefly appeared to become thoughtful. A colleague cleared his throat and dared to say, 'Is it because he is one metre eighty? Is that why?' From that time on I was known as One Metre Eighty. Whenever I arrived at a crime scene, the cry would

go up: 'One Metre Eighty is here, One Metre
Eighty is here.'

I am proud of my height. How many men
are depressed – even suicidal -because they are
short? My parents gave me a strong body and with
it came bright prospects. When I sat the police
academy entrance examination, they went easy on
me at the interview. At athletics meetings, I was
the one chosen to parade in front carrying the flag;
in college plays, I was usually the hero. Wherever I
went there were the openly admiring eyes of
female colleagues. For me, all this was quite
normal. My powerful physique was a gift from my
parents, and as far as I was concerned their gift
could never be repaid.

So when this case came along, I was lost. It
was a murder case. The murder victim was a
woman in her fifties, and the murder suspect
wasn't a stranger but none other than her own son.
This world has it all: shameless prostitutes, and a
son who kills his own mother. What a mess.

I was looking right at him: a disabled man.

As a kid he had suffered from polio, which explained the way he sat on the bed, his body twisted. I had someone help him up. Unexpectedly, as soon as he had been lifted, he slumped forward as if he was about to drop to the floor. His legs and feet had no strength to support him.

One of his neighbours, who was at the scene, said, 'You'll have to carry him out.' No one else could do it; only I was strong enough to move him to the car. Could a person like this really kill?

Another neighbour said, 'He rode everywhere on his mother's back. Even with a stick he couldn't stand up, so they threw the stick away.'

Well, I didn't see how he had managed to kill his mother. Couldn't his mother have just moved away? Most people have an instinct to save themselves. If she had shifted a little, he wouldn't have been able to get near her.

Maybe she hadn't had the heart. If she had moved, he would have fallen to the ground. A mother can't easily watch her son suffer a fall. She

had probably preferred to suffer herself. No doubt
this was why she had come to let her son kill her.
The murder weapon was a whip; her body was
covered with lash marks. Each lash, every single
one, had pushed her towards death. It was hard for
me to imagine how she could have endured that,
being flogged a step at a time closer to the final
point of life.

I inspected that whip. It was made of
leather, the real thing. It looked hard and dried up,
as if it had been soaked for a long time in water. I
didn't know how the murderer had got this. Even if
he had made it himself, he would have needed the
raw materials. How could he have got hold of them?
Everywhere he'd gone had been on his mother's
back. It seemed certain therefore that he'd obtained
this whip with his mother's help.

I noticed the whip's cotton sheath, which
had been custom-made to fit the handle. The sheath
had apparently been sewn together from a few rags
and something about its seams held my attention:
their very fine, intricate stitching. It was almost

14

impossible to detect the stitching at all. I felt it, and there was no sign of a join; it passed softly over my hand. Who had made this handle sheath? Was there another person in this case? If not, had the deceased herself made it?

The murderer still hadn't said a word.

2

The neighbours claimed that at the time of her murder the mother had called out once. Her swollen lungs had released a little air and then repressed the remainder. After that they heard nothing. Their door was closed. Some curious people went to the small adjoining grocery kiosk and put their ears to the wall. They heard the sound of a whip. No groans. When a person was being beaten to death, there should surely be some sound? But there was nothing and so it was impossible for them to confirm who was beating and who was being beaten.

The grocery store boss said, 'This is a cavity wall, there's only a thin layer of clapboard dividing the two rooms. If the wall was bare, we might have seen shadows.' But the wall was papered over and so it was impossible to see anything through it.

In recent weeks, no one had been to the house. Before, there had been a few incidents involving the mother and son, and they had asked their neighbours for help. Nothing like that recently though. The head of the residents' committee had knocked on their door and told the mother, 'If you need anything, then call us', but the mother had blocked the entrance to her home and just said: 'Need what?'

The neighbours said that a sour smell had seeped out from behind her body.

'Since she took that attitude, we didn't go there again,' the committee member said. 'We have plenty to keep us busy! Family planning, health and hygiene, rubbish collection, park construction, and our local song and dance troupe.

The song and dance troupe is the most satisfying. Whenever there's something going on, a festival, or the Sixteenth People's Congress, or some campaign, they get everyone going. The whole neighbourhood becomes lively. But all this had nothing to do with this house, because they kept themselves to themselves. They were good citizens though, they never caused any trouble. At least our committee didn't have to worry about them messing up the one-child policy. That man was never going to find a wife.'

There were just the two of them in their household: mother and son. The deceased's husband had passed on long ago. Widowed at the age of thirty, she had never married again because of her child. The mother and son were dependent on each other. The child contracted polio when he was just two years old. The experts insisted that there was no cure, but the mother devised her own treatment: she tied a wooden board to his feet, propped him up, and left him like that. At other times she lashed the child to the bedpost and let him hang there, writhing and twisting, to exercise his spinal column. She sometimes left him this way for five or six hours. People felt pity when they saw him in obvious pain, exhausted, beads of sweat trickling down his face. Surely his mother suffered too? But she forced the small child to keep doing this; in fact, he suffered beatings for not trying hard enough. Others attempted to intercede, and she said: 'If he doesn't do this now, what kind of life will he have later?' 'But will this do any good?' people asked. 'Good or not, we can't give up, we've got to keep trying,' she answered. The treatment ultimately made no difference at all to the child's legs.

The son was bright, the neighbours said. He hadn't gone to school, but he had quite a good vocabulary; he could read a few characters. Despite this he had no way to join normal society. People often saw the mother carrying her son. All through his childhood and even after reaching adulthood, she took him everywhere on her back, or else in her arms. As grown man of well over thirty, his mother still took him everywhere on her back, or else in her arms. Sometimes he embraced her neck, sometimes her waist; sometimes he even hung onto her breasts. One time he seemed about to slide out of her grasp and he seized hold of her breasts, like grabbing a safety bar.

What about bathroom visits? Had his mother helped him here too? One young guy had raised this question only to be shouted down. 'You lowlife! There's no need to mention that.' Everyone knew that the child slept in the same bed as his mother. No one felt that this was wrong. One disabled person and his mother; for survival. So what? Anyway, he had come from his mother's body, so how could he have inappropriate thoughts about that body? All people saw was a lonely, isolate, mother and her son.

The mother was a redundant factory worker. When her factory was sold, she was sent home with 10,000 yuan from the severment fund. Afraid of blowing that money, the mother put it in a savings account, and then found a part-time cleaning job with a private household. Each shift she earned 15 yuan. This work was convenient for her, because at lunchtime she could rush off to make food and look after her son. But she couldn't keep it up. Aged just fifty, her strength was already failing. As long as she was there, the son could have a life. But what if she wasn't there? Who could support him, take care of him? For this reason she decided that she had to find the son a wife.

The man she had cleaned for said, 'At first we couldn't think kind of wife her son could possibly have. We said that he should just forget about it. No one imagined that this disabled person had the right to get married.'

However, this man was actually the first one to introduce the woman's son to a potential bride. He did it at the mother's request, because she put so much into her job. She didn't just do clean the house, she washed his bowls and chopsticks. After a while, on her duty days, her employer didn't bother with the dishes, and left his clothes in a pile for her. But what kind of girl could he introduce to her son? For a long time he was puzzled. Of course the girl had to be physically normal, and she also couldn't be an idiot. She had to be able to look after the son. Aside from that, he decided the girl's appearance didn't really matter. Eventually he introduced the son to an ugly girl, a real fright. The girl had been warned beforehand that the son's legs and arms were a bit stiff, but had been led to believe that he could still manage to walk with a limp. She hadn't expected that he wouldn't even manage to stand in her presence. Immediately she told them to forget it.

There was no choice but to lower their standards. But what did 'lower' mean in this case? Uglier? Missing some vital feature (face, nose, eyes etc)? It was human nature to search for the higher thing, the employer reflected, but his job was to find someone ugly. Depressed, he wondered whether he might have better luck in the countryside. Finally he decided to travel to a village where people didn't have enough to eat.

There he might at least be able to select someone good-looking. When the son heard this, his mouth started to water.

'We have 10,000 yuan in our deposit book,' his mother said. 'Spend whatever's needed.' But her employer didn't use their money. Somehow, I don't know the full story, but with many twists and turns along the way, he brought a Sichuanese girl, who was very attractive, back to their house. She lived with them for a while and everyone said how nice she was. Then one day the mother staggered into the street yelling that their deposit book and even their ID cards were gone. That girl had taken them, along with the 10,000 yuan in their account. When they investigated, the girl turned out to be unknown at the address she had told them. They also learned that she was divorced. Everyone said, well, that's modern society. But modern society or not, nothing they said could make the son's situation seem less bleak. Even a divorced woman had left him.

Chen Xiwo

Afterwards, they put the word out that they would consider widows, they would consider women with children. Still no one was interested. Without that 10,000 yuan they didn't have a dowry; even a disabled girl was beyond their reach. No one could think of a single thing that would make any girl consider him.

The son started to resent his mother, and eventually to beat her. The mother was powerless. The neighbours said, as a mother you give your child everything, and your only fear is having nothing to give. A mother would cut flesh from her body for her son to eat. The neighbours couldn't bear to let her son beat her, and pleaded with them to stop. But the mother said, 'Let him. After he's beaten me for a while he feels better.' She offered her body to soak up his frustration.

Later she had simply shut the door on the world. When she did go out, she greeted the neighbours with a cheery good morning. Her smile made the bruises on her face even more noticeable. She went down the market for food because she had to cook for her son. No doubt that child had exhausted himself beating her and was hungry. If she didn't cook for him, her adored son might starve.

But no one had foreseen that she would be beaten to death.

3

One time, the mother came up with a crazy idea: she decided to barter herself for a daughter-in-law. This decrepit old guy lived a few streets away. He was so feeble that he didn't even complain about life any more; he couldn't really do anything. His wife had died, leaving him a retarded daughter. Not only was this daughter unable to take care of her father, she needed him to look after her. When upset, she would beat him. She beat him so hard that the father would stumble out into the street cursing furiously: 'Fuck your mum!'

Everyone would laugh and say: 'Haven't you already fucked her mum countless times?'

The old guy would smile and sigh: 'Yes, that's why I have this evil daughter. There's nothing I can do about it. If your daughter beats you, there's not a thing you can do.'

At some point the neighbours had mentioned this other household, and someone had joked that the two households seemed well-matched. Everyone laughed, but afterwards that mother really did launch an assault on the old man. It was well over the top.

She ran to the old guy's house and cooked for him, managed his household, humoured his simple daughter. Then she took her son round there on her back. While she got on with things there, her child was left to entertain the daughter. The son's body was deformed but there was nothing wrong with his brain. He didn't see that keeping such an idiotic girl company was much fun for him. The girl's IQ was barely at the level of a three year old. Everyone said, what would be achieved by this match? The stupid girl needed people to look after her. How could she look after a cripple? But the mother's reasoning was that after they had their own child, and the child had grown up, then he could look after his parents.

The old man revealed that the mother had made him an unexpected proposal. 'I will marry you, and then you can marry your daughter to my son. Our two families can live together and take care of each other.'

'Wasn't that prostitution?' some people said.

'No choice! It's unkind to say that,' others defended her.

'She was selling herself to get a grandchild,' a sympathetic person said.

Someone quipped that it would have been simpler for her just to have a grandchild with her son, but others protested that was too outrageous. People went to all kinds of lengths to have children; because they wanted to have children, their actions were not considered ridiculous.

The old guy hadn't even answered her proposal before the mother went ahead and moved her quilt down to his house. 'She climbed into the old guy's bed!' everyone said. Maybe it was tactical, but she didn't immediately make her son sleep with the daughter. Instead she put a mattress down on the floor. But that very night, her son was dragged out of there like a dead dog. It wasn't because he had assaulted the old man's daughter; the girl had no sexual awareness at all. He had come to play with her, and she was bored with him and wanted him to go. Because he couldn't move, she had dragged him out and left him in the middle of the road. A truck couldn't get by and the driver made a fuss, waking the whole street. All the windows opened and people looked out as the girl ran towards the immobile son shouting: 'Get lost, get lost. I don't want to play with you.'

No one knew whether to laugh or cry. The son crawled along the ground, his neck tense with the massive effort of trying to escape. But his mother blocked his path. She entreated that stupid girl, bowed down to her. No matter how she implored, the girl wouldn't give in: she demanded that they both left. In fact, it seemed that she had some basic smarts because she actually ran into a nearby telephone box and dialed 110. The cops showed up and, without bothering to sort out the facts, took the disabled son off in a car.

It was like he was being abducted, one eyewitness said. When the son didn't at once move as commanded, the cops lost patience and simply took him off. He thrashed about under the cop's arm, but his kicks were random. His feet struck out blindly, his eyes were full of despair. He could see his enemy, but his eyes lacked the ability to direct his movements.

He was quickly released but after that incident he became even more depressed. Everyone said that the door of their house was always locked.

Interrogation

1

As a crime squad detective, I was used to difficult suspects. Some denied everything. Some faked stupidity; others, honesty. But I had never before encountered someone who completely ignored me. Because of his condition, he often had to contort his face to look at people. His eyes met you obliquely, filled with an almost terrifying glare. At that moment, though, his stare was fixed slightly to one side of us, making him seem aloof. It was as though his consciousness had flown away. He was preoccupied, perhaps, with matters in another world. Was it that he had killed his mum and his spirit had followed her? Or was his life now something of little value to him?

Having him in residence was a challenge for the jail. He couldn't take care of himself. He needed help to eat; he couldn't crawl onto his bed to sleep. Sure you could make him lie on the ground, but then what about when he needed to piss or shit? He didn't have any close relatives. There was nothing to do but ask the jail cleaners to help him. Because this wasn't part of their usual duties, they made a fuss. Once though, I met a cleaner emerging from his cell after she had helped the suspect to go to the toilet, and she said conspiratorially, 'Aiya, that guy's cock is really big.'

I was surprised by this because I had never thought of him as a sexual being. After all, though, he was a thirty-four-year-old man.

But his cock hardly seemed relevant. My concern was how to pry open his mouth. I needed the truth; I needed his confession. I decided to secretly keep him under close surveillance, especially at night, when people often shed some of their armour. Sure enough, that very night I found him restless. He lay on the floor of the holding cell in the dark. He writhed about, banging his head against the wall. His face was turned

towards the inside of the cell so that I could only
see his back, which twitched slightly. Maybe he
was sobbing. A person who had killed his mother,
whatever the circumstances, would surely
experience agonising remorse. He couldn't avoid
feeling responsible. I heard him call out, 'Mum!'
Was he repentant? But his voice seemed rather to
be full of aggression. His body struggled even
more frantically. He looked like a trapped animal,
desperately struggling. Then suddenly his whole
body shook in a violent spasm. It was like he had
been shot. After that, he didn't move any more and
was as still as the dead. What on earth could this
mean?

After an age, he turned his body round. To
be exact, he first propped himself up on one arm
and then flopped painfully over. My impression
was that he was looking for something but was
unable to find it. Blindly he sought it everywhere.
The moon stole in through a high window and
illuminated a face full of loss, unrecognizable from
the lifeless countenance he had presented these

past few days. This face was aroused, or just
coming down from the peak of arousal. I was
shocked and amazed.

What had happened to his body? By the
look of it, he still hadn't found what he wanted.
Eventually he stretched out a hand and rubbed the
wall. What did he imagine was there? The
detention room was dark, and the moonlight didn't
reach the walls, so I couldn't see what was going
on. Finally he lay down once again and let out a
long sigh. To me it sounded like the moan of a
wild animal after it had been satisfied.

Something occurred to me and I hurried
away.

2

He had been smearing his semen on the wall. I was
revolted of course.

I made my discovery when I entered his
cell after the disabled suspect was taken to court
for examination. I had never before considered that

a criminal or even a suspect had any right to gratification. In prison men and women were often locked up together. Cells lacked privacy; everything was on display. How did they deal with the call of the flesh? Before they were locked up, sex was part of their lives. But from the day they came in here, it went unmentioned. This substance smeared on the wall before my face reminded me that prisoners were still human beings. They were human beings the same as me. I felt uncomfortable, and I had this feeling that the suspect was very close to me. I could smell his sticky breath, and he and I had the same smell. That smell was the smell of men's sex.

I tried not to think about it. I had never really confronted my sexual nature before; I had just known that I was a cop. Now it seemed that I had been exposed. I was revealed to myself, and so I was angry. I wanted to shout out, to prove that I was different from him. But I convinced myself that my indignation was a result of his behaviour: a murderer, he was completely unrepentant, and now he did this!

I went straightaway to the court to start the examination.

Q: What did you do last night?

No answer: he raised his head and fixed me with a penetrating gaze.

Q: You dare to say that you did nothing?

A: Nothing? (His lips twitched and the words slipped out. Finally he had broken his silence!) Nothing. What am I supposed to have done?

Q: I'm asking you.

A: I didn't do anything!

Q: You didn't? Then what's that on the wall?

A: Nothing.

Q: You still say nothing? I just went in your cell. What did I find there?

Grin.

Q: What is that substance?

A: Snot.

Q: You're lying! Let me remind you of government policy: honesty results in lenience, but defiance has serious consequences! You must explain honestly.

A: Explain what?

Q: You should know.

A: I don't.

'You lie! You were playing with yourself. There, you've forced me to say it.' I felt sick.

The other's head dropped, but he still obstinately said, 'No, no, I didn't do it.'

Q: No? Didn't do what?

That gaze flashed over my face like lightning, then withdrew. It was too bad that his eyes couldn't follow the commands of his brain; they were two broken wheels being dragged along in the wake of his thoughts. His throat pulsed dramatically with emotion, making me think that I had been too cruel. But I had to be firm.

'What didn't you do?' I pressed him.

'I didn't touch it.'

'Touch what?'

'Didn't touch.'

'Touch where?'

The meaning was clear to all present. Admittedly this was humiliating for him, but I had the advantage and I needed him to say it. The only way he could prevail was if he refused to speak again. But it seemed now that he couldn't be silent any more. The scab had been peeled off and it was dripping with fresh blood. He couldn't seal the wound. He stared at me and his head jerked about like he was a chicken that was being strangled. Finally he got mad.

'Don't think that you are so great!' he said. 'Don't imagine there is anything special about you just because you have a healthy body.'

'Nothing special about me at all. All I am is an officer of the law,' I answered seriously.

'Ha! Officer of the law? If you were like me, could you enforce the law?'

'Even if I wasn't a law officer, I would be a law-abiding citizen.'

'And if you were disabled?'

'Even if I were, I would still live in a decent way. I wouldn't murder people.'

'You don't have the right to say that.'

'Why?'

'You're not me, and you're not my mother.'

'Aren't we talking about your mother? Did she want you to murder her? No one wants to be murdered, and sons should not kill their mothers. Why did you want to kill your own mother?'

'We couldn't live together.'

'Wasn't your mother your only support?'

'I didn't need her support.'

'You felt angry with her?'

'I hated her.'

'Why? Because she couldn't save you from being disabled?'

'Right!' He suddenly looked emotional.

I was delighted, because I felt confident that he would soon give something away. But he calmed down and didn't say anything more. He propped himself up as if he wanted to leave, but he shook and basically couldn't rise. As he slid down to the ground, he cried out agonizingly.

'Okay, you can go,' I said.

His gaze sought the cop who had brought him here. After I waved my hand, the cop came to pick him up. The murder suspect crawled towards him like an impatient child, suggesting none of the pain that he had apparently felt a minute ago. He seemed in a desperate hurry to drag himself out. The cop scooped him up. As they left, I watched him.

'You hated her, didn't you?', I shouted after him. 'Is it because she stopped you doing what you did last night?'

He nearly slid off the back of the cop who was carrying him. His head turned painfully and looked in my direction.

'Sex is a basic need,' I continued, 'but you and your mum lived in a single room.'

The cop sensed where this was going and carried the suspect back into the room; the suspect's expression was despairing.

'You two were always together,' I said.

He suddenly laughed. 'What do you mean, always together? Do you think it is impossible that we were apart?' he said unexpectedly.

'There must have been times,' I conceded, 'but how did you deal with your cum?'

He clammed up.

'Did your mother find out about your disgusting habit?'

'What is so disgusting?' he said. 'In your eyes, everything is disgusting.'

'So your mother permitted it?'

'I don't permit you to smear her.'

'I am not smearing, this is an interrogation. A solemn interrogation. You must answer my questions. Okay, I'll ask you another. What did your mother think about this? How did she react?'

He didn't answer.

'Your silence says it all. She hated it, and so you killed her!' I said. Of course, this reasoning was a bit of a stretch. I just wanted to provoke him.

'I didn't hate her!' he said. 'I didn't hate my mum!'

He shook from head to toe as he glared furiously at me. If it wasn't that he couldn't control his body, he would probably have flung himself on me and beaten me to death. But he could only cry out, shout himself hoarse, choke with resentment. His eyeballs bulged as if they might pop out. Why such a strong reaction? Perhaps he really had loved his mother; in which case, why had he killed her? Or maybe he hadn't meant to kill his mother, just beat her. Maybe her death had really been an accident.

3

He apparently realized that resistance was useless and stopped fighting. Gasping for breath, he slumped back in his chair, his face turned to the ceiling. It looked as if his head had been half severed by the back of the chair and was dangling there.

'You hated her,' I said. 'You hated your mother, and so you killed her.'

He didn't protest.

'Because she gave birth to you?'

He nodded. 'If she couldn't make me happy, why have me?' he said.

'You're mad!' I said. 'Your illness happened when you were two years old. You had already been born.'

'She could have strangled me.'

'What?'

'She could have killed me then!' He laughed insanely. 'I was too young to understand death. I was so small. One nip and that would have been it.'

'Don't talk nonsense.'

'End it,' he continued. 'Once you have grown up and become stronger, it is harder to die.'

'Don't think so much about death.'

'You live such an easy life, no wonder you don't think of death. Whatever you want, you can have. You can have a wife.'

'You can too,' I said, maybe a bit
illogically. It was that kind of logic where you just
hope to comfort someone regardless of the facts.

'Yes, I can' he said. He started laughing
again. 'But what kind of trash would that be?' he
shouted. 'This world's ugly and stupid women;
I've met them all. It opened my eyes. What would
be the point for me of marrying one of them? I
didn't want to get married, but Mother said, "You
should get married; this is what normal people do."
But as I am not a normal person why should I be
made to do what they do?'

'You don't want to get married?'

'Don't want.'

'You don't need to?'

'Don't need.'

'Really?'

He looked at me, his face distorted in an
evil way. 'I can jerk off!' he said unexpectedly.
That surprised me. Apparently he had a malicious
mind. 'Have you ever jerked off?' he asked me.

I was dumbfounded. I had done often, of course, in my bachelor days. Everyone has jerked off, just like every driver has violated some traffic regulation. But to his face I lied. I am a cop, I couldn't admit to that.

'That's because you have women,' he said. 'Others do that for you!'

'Don't talk nonsense,' I bellowed.

'Aren't you a man as well?' He laughed. 'Our only difference is circumstances.'

'Still talking nonsense!' I shouted. Once again I had used that same phrase 'talking nonsense', and so it seemed that my powers of expression were limited.

'Is it a good feeling,' he asked, 'to fuck girls?' He was provoking me.

'Ask yourself!'

'Very good,' he said. 'Really too good. Ah, that this world has such joy.'

After he said that, I felt on edge. Eventually I calmed down, but my body had a numb feeling, like I had just woken from a trance.

I Love My Mum

'Did you always deal with your urges this way?' I asked.

'Not to start with,' he said.

'So how did you?'

'Wet dreams,' he said.

'When did they start?'

'That night that your colleagues from 110 arrested me,' he said. 'That was the first time. Can you imagine? That night after they had dropped me home, my mind raced. Finally I slipped into a dreamless sleep; there were never any dreams.'

I nodded. I hadn't expected that he would say so much.

'In the middle of the night I woke with an erection. It was as if my hard-on had woken me. What could I do? Without dreams, I had only reality. But what did I have, in reality? My life was empty. Nothing except for this room, this bed. But the bed wasn't empty, because my mother was in it, and I ... startled her. I won't say any more.'

'I know,' I said.

'You know what?'

'I know that you had to share a bed with your mother,' I said.

He laughed, apparently very embarrassed.

'No big deal,' I said.

'No big deal? My mother. Would I really do my own mother?' he said.

I was startled. To mention sex and your own mother in the same sentence, however casually, was to violate a taboo. Actually it was nauseating. Why had he said that? What had he meant?

'When your mother caught you doing that, it must have been embarrassing,' I suggested.

'Yes.'

'She caught you then?'

'Maybe I woke her up. She had words with me.'

'Just "words".'

'Yes, "words",' he retorted, looking at me wildly. 'If not "words", what else?' His raised voice had changed its tone.

I had meant to suggest that he was playing things down, using the phrase "had words" when he actually meant "curse". I hadn't expected this reaction. What didn't he want me to discover?

'Tell me exactly what she said.'

'Okay, it wasn't "say", it was "beat".'

'Beat?' I was puzzled by this. How had we got back to beating?

'Yes, "beat"!' he said. 'Do you understand hate?' He laughed abruptly. 'Do you like to watch violence? You cops are all voyeurs. Okay, I'll tell you what happened. My mother said that I wasn't human, that I was an animal! She beat me like an animal. Yes, I am not a human being, I am an animal. *You* are a human being. Or are you? Let's swap places and we'll see. What if you woke up in the middle of the night, alone? No one there, only your mum. Only a mother. No women you could use. You would use your mum!'

'What?!'

The other suddenly seemed to come to his senses. 'Forgive me, talking nonsense,' he said.

He had used that very same phrase 'talking nonsense'. On the surface, then, our vocabularies were similarly lacking. When we fear the truth, this phrase 'talking nonsense' is a good deflector. For him to come out with that, there had to be something behind it. Those who commit terrible crimes must suffer in a spiritual wasteland. He was doing his best to escape from that wasteland, but he had betrayed himself. Could it be that something had happened? I simply didn't dare to imagine what. But as a cop, it was sometimes my duty to confront unpleasant things.

'No, you're not "talking nonsense",' I said with cruel directness.

'Really?' he said. He laughed and suggested that I was joking. Because his illness had made him twitchy, his laugh had a nervous quality.

'No joke!' I ruthlessly insisted. 'We have investigated.'

'Investigated what?'

'You know.'

'I know what?' he said. He laughed:

'What?'

'No walls are impenetrable.'

'Walls?'

'If I must spell it out, the walls of your house are thin,' I said.

I felt myself that this tactic was unfair, but I was a cop. It was necessary for the interrogation, even if it was slightly cruel.

'She cursed me,' he said. 'She was too embarrassed to even refer to it directly. She just said "that thing". It seemed like she didn't mean anything in particular, but I understood. Mother knew. For your own mother to know about this part of your life; it's hard to describe the shame. But what choice did I have, even though I knew the consequences? The most dangerous time was three in the morning; suddenly waking when everything was dark. Dark traps you in the here and now, alone with your desires. Then there was the next day, being cursed by Mother again, and later the beatings. I am a man who has never left his mother's breast. Perhaps for this reason, Mother felt that I was still a child and that beating me was no big deal. But I was no longer a child. I felt hate!'

'So this was why you killed her?'
I had almost said it out loud. It was an easy inference, a logical one. I had got what I wanted. But for some reason I hesitated. If this was all there was to it, then why was the suspect so flustered? I wasn't certain, and so I continued to question him.

'Was hate the only reason?'
'What else?' he asked me in reply.
'You tell me,' I said. 'Let me repeat that our law is lenient to those who cooperate, but strict with those who resist. The facts are known, but we can still decide how to deal with this. I don't think that your mother would want her son executed, even though you beat her. No mother wants her son dead.'

His head dropped.
'Think about it. You beat your mother, but she didn't resist. Why?'

'How do you know that?'

'If she had resisted, could you have beaten her? Could you have left bruises on every part of her body?'

He appeared shocked. 'How do you know?'

'What?'

'Her body was bruised.'

I laughed. 'We have pathologists. We have to do an autopsy,' I said, 'according to procedure.'

'You had no right to do that!' he said. 'She is my mum!'

I laughed. 'You murdered her! Is she still your mum?'

'Anyway, you had no right,' he insisted.

He wanted to stand, but once again he rocked and fell back. Those around him quickly supported him. He pushed them violently away. He seemed determined to crawl out of there on his own, but it was agonizingly difficult. There was no strength in his legs, and the strength in his arms was severely limited. Still he crawled.

'Where is my mum? Where is my mum? You had no right to move her! You had no right to do an autopsy!' He shouted himself hoarse, beat the floor.

I was astonished. Why was the guy so touchy about an autopsy?

3

I ordered a second autopsy.

There was semen inside the vagina. After tests, this substance turned out to be none other than her son's. Shock! I was truly stunned.

I raced to his cell, thrust the test results at him. He scrunched up the paper in his hand, as if afraid that others might see it. I wanted it back, but he wouldn't give it up. He even tried to stuff it in his mouth.

'It's useless,' I said. 'We know!'

He froze, as if dead. But even if he had really died, that wouldn't have helped him. He had to accept society's damning judgment. There was no way now that he could avoid that.

'When?' I asked him.

'After she died,' he said.

'She was already dead?'

'Yes; she'd left me. What was I to do?'

'Do about what?' I was dumbfounded. 'I bet this was going on for a long time.'

'You don't know how hard it was,' he said, 'being woken in the night by my hard-on. No one to lend a hand. I had to help myself, even if it meant taking all Mother's curses, all her beatings. After Mother found me out, it was as humiliating as if I'd been stripped naked, my face ripped off. My life was over. But that thought released me. Everything seemed different, a burden had lifted. I was naked and shameless, free to indulge myself! I couldn't stop touching myself. I did it to my heart's content, imagining a girl's body, the way her hole felt. That body was a fantasy; I couldn't really feel it. What was a woman's body like? No idea. Never seen one. I had only seen my mum.

When she showered, she pulled across a plastic curtain. After washing, she usually dressed before coming out; sometimes, though, because she hadn't completely buttoned up, some of her breast might show. Or when we went to sleep, she would expose a little. One night a button was undone and I glimpsed her belly. Can you picture that? I had to see more, to satisfy my imagination, and so I drew back the cover. As I had suspected, Mother's jacket was slightly open and had risen up. The lower part of her breast was visible, the last third of the moon. Seeing that felt like someone had stuck a needle in my eyes.

'The next day, though, I had to see again. I couldn't stop myself. I tried to force myself not to, but it was useless. This was a woman's body: right there beside me, a real woman's body. The woman was older, but what did that matter? In my situation I should crave the ugliest of women, right? The stupidest? What did it matter if she was somewhat older? She was better-looking than my previous matches. My mum was a beauty. You

have seen her. Even dead, she is stunning. Why
should I seek far and wide? Why make life hard?
Why turn from beauty and look for ugliness?
Where's the logic in that!'

I said, 'Yet again you are twisting logic.
This wasn't any woman, it was your mother! Could
you really do it with your mother?'

'I borrowed her.' He smiled cunningly.
'Just used her for a bit.'

'What?'

'Is there anything so bad about that?' he
said. 'Make do with what you have.' He even went
as far as to say that. 'And she wouldn't have got
pregnant,' he said. 'Past that age.'

Incredible!

'For you this sounds strange,' he said,
'because well-fed people don't understand famine.
Those who have enough food to eat can afford a
sense of shame. But that's not me! You wouldn't
consider eating crumbs off the street, you would
worry about hygiene. You would say, "Who does
the cleaning around here?'

'Maybe.'

'Once upon a time there was a shipwreck. No rescuers came, and there was nothing to drink or eat. A few people on the boat died of hunger, and it seemed like the rest would soon go the same way. Some suggested eating the corpses. Others said, how could they eat human flesh? Even dead, they were still people! But why not? For them, life was over. Remember that I am talking about eating the dead, not the living. Why not eat? It was only necessary to regard them as any beast's flesh: sustenance. The alternative was for everyone to starve while the flesh that could save their lives rotted. Was that sensible? A woman's body; a famished man; use what you've got: what's wrong with it?'

'There's morality,' I said.

'Morality?' He laughed coldly. 'Morality is for those who have enough. Remember, though, that most of us can never have enough, even the rich. There were two kinds of people on that boat: those who did what they had to, and those who became food so that others could live. Which kind of person would you have been?'

I was taken back. Which kind? Maybe morality is a fantasy, only meaningful when contemplating spiritual matters. But how often do we think about our souls? We prefer to continue on our individual paths to destruction. Sure, the only way to get by in this world is to be flexible. How far, though, should this flexibility go?

'Did your mother agree?' I asked.

'Of course not!' he said at once. 'How could she?'

It was impossible, of course. I thought that too, or I wanted to.

'So that was why she beat you?' I asked.

'Yes, she beat me,' he said. 'She held me up and beat me.'

He said that she had beaten him even harder than ever before.

'I held my mother like a drowning man clings onto a lifebuoy. This person who beat me was the one who had saved my life. I couldn't

56

leave her! I suddenly felt that I had noone else to rely on except for the one who beat me. I held my mother and cried loudly. At that moment I felt regret.'

'At that moment?'

'It passed.'

'That was it?' I said.

He admitted that later he had felt guilty again.

There was more, I thought. I imagined that scene: the mother beating her son but unable to cast him out. Beating him would have been like beating herself. Still, no one could beat themselves to death, any more than it was possible to grab hold of one's hair and pull oneself up off the ground.

'How did she die?' I said.

'I beat her to death,' he answered. There was no hesitation.

He said that she had made him beat her. 'Mother said, "You beat me, never mind. If you beat me to death then I won't know anything more."'

'So you really did beat her to death?'

'Yes,' he said.

'But surely your mother couldn't really have wanted to die?'

He lowered his head and I realized that this was a stupid remark. No one wanted to die. But the victim was dead alright. This man surely felt deep regret, yet there was no way to undo what he had done.

'Was it an accident?' I asked.

There were no witnesses to the crime. As someone who hasn't experienced many setbacks in his life, I find it easy to feel sympathy for others. Perhaps because I am shallow, I easily feel a shallow sympathy.

But his answer came as a surprise: 'No.'

Life was unimportant to him. He wanted to join his mother, but had no way to kill himself, and so he wanted to use us to achieve his objective. Well, I wasn't going to be used.

'Let me ask you a specific question,' I said. 'Where did that whip come from?'

'Bought.'

'By whom?'

'My mum.'

I exhaled coldly. That whip, that whip with the soft cotton handle sheath.

'When you bought the whip, did it have that sheath?'

'No, it was made later.'

'Who made it?'

'My mum,' he answered. 'She searched for a long time before she found that cloth. She said that cotton towel would be softer on my hands.' I suddenly felt emotion. 'So she did love you,' I said to him. 'You loved her too. Right?'

He didn't answer.

'Remember, you have committed a crime,' I said. 'At your trial, you must tell all.'

Confession

1

Being a nice guy is great. There's satisfaction to be had from good deeds. Nice guys are mostly happy. But not me. I'm a prisoner. If the law lets me off, if I am released, it won't make any difference. I am a prisoner of my body, and that's a life sentence.

This world is slippery and people use that to resolve tricky situations. They will forgive crimes. You repent; I forgive you. This is because they find those same crimes in their own hearts. They are afraid, and forgive so that they can escape their fears.

I sat in the interrogation room. The clerk took up a pen and looked at me. I had only to open my mouth and his pen would record all that I said. Most crooks lied to the cops. The consequences of honesty could be severe. They had dropped hints. I had got the message. I could say that the murder was an accident. You are being good to me, I will cooperate. It was unintended, a moment of confusion, like lots of things. Find reasons, muddy the waters. Was the system to blame? If not the system, was society in a mess? Did you do this thing because bad people blocked your way; you couldn't find work? If you were an intellectual, they might even allow that your act of rebellion was excusable. But I wasn't a rebel. Were things ever that simple? Revolt was like bathing: your body felt great afterwards, but you couldn't get rid of cancer cells by washing. Not even by chemotherapy.

Even if you are not disabled, you can always find excuses.

But hadn't I always hated being disabled? Hadn't I always said that if only I wasn't disabled then I would be married, happy. Oh, I was weak. I complained that I was unlucky, and had come to believe that whatever I wanted was denied me. After the cops had brought me home that time, I had woken in the middle of the night. Mother was

roused too by my sobbing. She embraced me,
rubbed my face, put my head in her bosom. She
wasn't wearing much, just a nightgown. Cheap
sleep clothes have the texture of everyday family
life. Mother's chest was soft, like those waterbeds
in adverts. I could smell her oyster. Maybe to other
people that smell is sour, but I liked it because that
was the smell of our house. That smell had always
been there. If it wasn't, then I would have felt that
something was lost to me. When I was small,
Mother's body had constantly stunk of sweat. She
would lift her clothes to give me milk from her
exposed sweating breasts. That night I longed to
guzzle Mother's milk again like a little pig. My
legs felt numb like they were wrapped in bandages.
My arms, my whole body, were the same:
paralyzed.

I said: 'Mum, I want to drink your milk.'
Mother laughed. 'Stupid child, talking nonsense.
Drinking your mother's milk at your age. Wouldn't
you feel ashamed?'

'I'm serious,' I said.

Mother seemed to realize that something was wrong. She broke away from me. 'That's enough! I know that you have suffered,' she said. 'Sleep; tomorrow I'll start looking again.'

I knew this meant that she would look for a wife for me. But did I want that, I asked myself.

The answer was: no.

That frightened me.

After that I dared not look at Mother.

I knew what this meant also.

In the evening, I climbed alone onto the bed. I saw Mother's silhouette through the mosquito net chasing a mosquito. The net billowed and her silhouette moved with it. Instantly I closed my eyes. Mother joined me and I deliberately shifted to the far side of the bed. I was showing her my hurt, and yet it seemed strange that I'd never had these kinds of feelings before. Mother went to sleep. For me, there was no sleep. I softly turned and looked at her back, which faced me. I found that Mother wasn't really old. Her body was not that of an old woman. Perhaps because she hadn't had more

children after me, or because she always worked
hard and didn't eat much, she was slim. Whenever
she leaned forward it looked like her waist had
snapped in half; you wanted to reach out and touch
it.

Trying to stay calm, I touched myself, and
waited for a crack to appear in her clothes. But that
night her clothes were sealed tight. It was as if she
had taken special precautions, and so I had to rely
solely on my imagination to bring myself off. The
next day I was afraid Mother would find out what
I'd done. There was no way to deny it; better to kill
myself, but I had no way to do that. It seemed that
Mother didn't find out though. At least my pants
weren't wet.

The next night, the same thing. The third
night, the fourth. Gradually I felt dissatisfied. I
moved closer to Mother's body, bumped against it.
Indistinctly I felt that body recoil. But Mother
didn't wake. I became braver and pressed nearer.
She slept on. I put my leg on her body and at once

felt giddy. Still she didn't wake. How could she be in such a deep sleep?

I came on her body. My cum glistened there brightly. At the same time I called out: 'Mum.'

The body stirred slightly. But didn't rouse. It was as if she was dead. I actually hoped that she was dead, and that after this was done I could die too. I was satisfied now.

Very gently, I wiped my semen from Mother's body.

The next morning she got up. At first it seemed like she hadn't discovered anything, but she had a shower. She never usually showered in the mornings. Could it be that she knew what had happened? She washed her sleep clothes, but she washed them all, including ones that hadn't been soiled by me. I relaxed again. After that she continued with her usual chores, cooked the rice, prepared a few dishes for me. She gave me my meal and told me to eat first while she returned to

the stove. But there were no more dishes to cook.
Instead she cleared up.

I said, 'Wash all the plates together when
you have eaten.' She didn't reply.

I shouted: 'Ma!'

'Don't call me Ma!' she said. For a moment
she looked mad, but then she turned remorseful
and started to fuss about her work. She even put
clean bowls into the sink to wash. I understood
though. It was impossible for Mother not to have
known what I was doing. How naive I'd been.
Blinded by lust!

In the middle of things, I had called out
'Ma' very loudly. Unavoidable. It had just slipped
off my tongue. I was with her all day long, calling
out 'Ma' very often. For me it was a natural term
of affection, easy just to blurt out. Maybe, though,
I'd always had those feelings for my mum, because
Mother was the most beautiful woman in the world.
Those girls she had tried to match me with were
trash in comparison! Thinking of girls, I
remembered how once my mother had carried me

to a department store. Her back had ached and, as there hadn't been any other place for me, she had just sat me on top of a counter. The female shop assistant swore at my mother. She looked young, but was made up like a tart, with pencil eyebrows. What right did this kind of girl have to swear at Mother? I was furious. Well, I didn't want her for my wife. Of course people might say, she wouldn't want you anyway! But really I didn't. It wasn't just because girls like that didn't want me. Basically, I was picky. I didn't want to get married. When that idiot girl treated me that way, I couldn't take it. It was I who had rejected her. The whole situation had just been too humiliating. I know, in this age my kind of attitude is unfashionable. Everyone is mercenary; even well-off people act like beggars. Cash is king. Well, I didn't want to beg. I wanted my mum! I loved my mum!

2

One night, Mother suggested that we go for a walk.
She carried me on her back to a district far from
our home. We passed a massage establishment and
Mother said that perhaps a massage might help my
condition. Inside, the whole place was painted red
and there were women whose blurred faces
contrasted with their luridly exposed flesh. I had
never been to this kind of place before, but I
guessed what it was. A TV news report about the
war on vice had once said that in our city,
immorality was the biggest driver of economic
growth. You know that well, Captain, right?

A girl led us into this small inner room.
There was a smell of damp mixed with perfume
and cigarettes. These smells had nothing to do with
me. I didn't smoke, I wasn't a real man, and so I
had no right to be with women who wore perfume.

At the girl's suggestion, Mother put me
down on a massage table and said that she was
going shopping. She looked meaningfully at the
girl and then left without saying anything else.
Because of that look I realized that Mother had

already talked with the girls, and had brought me
here with something in mind. She hadn't been
asleep that night; she had known everything. But
how had she thought this up? How was she willing
to spend the money? Maybe it was like she had
said once: when you have to spend, don't stint. In
her view, she had no choice. So things had come to
this; after this, what else was forbidden? Anyway
this was all about getting release. Here is a hole;
use it for a while. What is bad about that? How
many clients of prostitutes are, in their own way,
good husbands, good fathers, good and responsible
at their jobs, good citizens? They wouldn't bomb
buildings or kill innocents. Realistically, this was
nothing so bad. Why not do it?

    The girl touched me. She didn't ask me
what I wanted; my impression was that Mother had
arranged everything. The girl put her hand on my
leg. It was like being struck by lightning: a woman!
Her hand felt soft, I admitted. She was very young.
I had never before encountered such a soft, young
girl. Maybe she thought that I would touch her, but

when she discovered that I did not, without any fuss she untied her clothes. I saw a body even more nubile and lovely than her hand. I confess that I nearly lost control.

That hole! The promised land I had dreamed of.

My pants came off and my cock was standing up like a rifle. At last I could be a soldier, throw myself into battle.

She knew that I couldn't stand and so she slithered on top of my body. Her movements were soft, like a snake. She licked my nipple, and then she stood and manipulated me with her hand, moved me towards herself. That hole! I was just about to go inside! Use for a minute! Sink in, use for a minute!

But was this what I needed?

I jerked and the girl fell off the narrow bed. She looked at me, very puzzled at first, and then indignant. Yes, I deserved her anger. She hadn't wronged me; she hadn't done anything wrong. It was me. My fault! I couldn't ... not this way.

When Mother returned, the girl said to me,
'If your mother hadn't spoken to us before...'
Mother's face reddened and she mumbled, 'So it's
this kind of messed-up place! Let's go,' she said,
very embarrassed. I knew she was lying to save
face. 'I thought it was a legitimate massage place,'
she said. 'I am really stupid.'

Mother was always eager to excel, and
never confessed when she had screwed up. Even
years ago when her daft plan to strengthen my
lower body completely failed, she never admitted
defeat. But now she had actually volunteered that
she was stupid. Oh, Mother! I understand: next to
shame and disgrace, what does stupidity amount to?
Anyway, even if you had no choice but to admit
that you planned this, what is prostitution
compared with incest? No more than an extra pair
of chopsticks at a banquet. It's what happens when
you swim in polluted waters, but for some reason I
could not swim. Surprisingly, I was a non-
swimmer.

Those girls weren't wrong. A person like
me, a disabled man, still had needs. The whole
world is rotten; was I going to change that? Who
was I to be so principled? It cracks me up! I don't
think of myself as sexually conservative. I just
wanted to have, to get, love. This was no one's
business other than my own. Maybe you will say it
also concerned another? But that other was my
mum, who would make any sacrifice for me. She
was willing to give herself to that decrepid old man
in exchange for a wife for me, so why not give
herself to me? The person who would give me
everything, the one who loved me most.

I wanted to love my mum. This wasn't
about a hole. It had no relation to the mouse hole
beneath the cooker. It had nothing in common with
the hole in the broken straw mat. Those were
artificial holes unfit to contain my spirit. The sky
was dark, the lamps were lit. Mother had got into
bed. She slept. My spirit had finally found its home.
I wanted to go inside, deep inside.

Even I was shocked by myself. What was going on?

My mother pretended to sleep. Most likely she knew what I wanted, but didn't know how to stop me. I read the flicker of her eyelid as a sign of her mind's inner turmoil. Maybe she had never thought that it would come to this, so quickly. Her back was to me, immobile. I removed her sleep pants. She seemed to resist a bit, but didn't turn over. If she had turned, the situation would have been forced into the open. Maybe she thought that if she let me just have a look, a touch, that would satisfy me. Mother was always the optimist. But my courage grew.

I wanted to go to hell.

I wanted to go straight there.

I entered her.

She trembled, but the movement was very slight. She shifted, but then seemed to still be unconscious, as if she had just moved in her sleep. Her new position actually made it more convenient for me. While she slept, I got on with things very comfortably. I half wondered whether she knew. She was deliberately letting me have my way and use her for a bit. No big deal. She was pretending not to know so that the whole thing could be kept in the dark. Or was she pretending to herself that I was another man? That dying old man? I could also have imagined that I was with another woman. But I didn't. The woman I wanted was this one. I called out: 'Ma!'

My call came as quite a surprise. Did I want to wake her? She must have heard. Even though my call hadn't been loud, I was very close, and the night was quiet. But she didn't stir. That told me finally that she was faking. A car approached outside, and she stirred slightly in her apparently deep sleep and her body moved. If she heard the car outside, how was it possible that she couldn't hear my voice?

Why wake her? I wanted this person. It was the person I loved, not a hole. Not flesh. If my desire was for flesh, why not visit whores? What difference was there between two female bodies?

Because it was this person, though, my mother, I felt that this was different. I wanted to liberate these feelings, this truth. Even if I was confused, even if Mum's eyes were shut, we could get by like this. My problem was solved; she could feign ignorance. No big deal. It was just making use of her for a bit, that was all. In this world, few face up to their own crimes. Even though countless crimes are committed, in this era we urgently need to acknowledge our own misdeeds. But my mother was too timid, determined not to wake.

Eventually I couldn't keep going any longer.

I ejaculated.

At once I felt a bitter flood of remorse.

The next morning, I said to her leadingly: 'Ma [I still deliberately called her Ma, but as soon as I said it my body went numb], last night you slept very deeply.'

She looked at me blankly. 'Yes,' she said. 'I was very tired yesterday.'

'Really?' I said. 'If there had been an earthquake, would you have woken?'

Again a blank expression, and then a despairing one. 'Well, if I am dead, then I am dead,' she said abruptly.

'If you were dead, what would I do?'

'So I really need to find you a wife,' she said. She hadn't mentioned that for a long time.

'Find who? That stupid girl?' I asked, deliberately being caustic.

She smiled sadly: 'Mother will find you the best one.'

'That is you,' I said sincerely. 'Mum is the best!'

'What nonsense are you talking. Eat! When you've finished I need to go out. I don't have time to talk nonsense with you. Nonsense.'

Mother saying 'nonsense' was her way of covering things up. Maybe I really shouldn't have tried to expose her; it was too cruel.

She didn't even eat after that, just ran out in a big fluster. After she had gone, I noticed a roll of toilet tissue on the bed. This was something that had never been there before. Her clothes were also arranged there; both upper and lower body, outer and inner garments, in the form of a person. My mother. I threw myself on the pile, touched it, sniffed it. I wrapped the clothes around me. I was deliriously happy; I came again.

Mother returned soon after. She dealt smoothly with the paper and the clothes. Quite casually, she put the clothes back in the cupboard, as if to cover up that there was anything unusual about them. Sometimes Mother was really funny.

I said, 'Ma!'

'What?'

'Come here a minute.'

'Why?' she said.

'I need to piss,' I said.

She hesitated, but as there was no choice she brought over the chamber pot. She stood the pot at my feet, and helped me off the bed while I leaned on her; then she opened my trousers.

I flung my arms around her.

This wasn't a sleeping embrace, it was eyes wide open. In broad daylight we faced each other. 'You can't go straight to sleep?' she asked, and then she trembled and pushed me away. I fell to the ground.

I had no way to get up. You see, dear readers, I am disabled. She helped me. I stood uncertainly, and she had no choice but to hold me again.

Once again I hugged her.

She lashed out at me. Maybe she did so too wildly, because she slipped and fell. I wanted to help her up. But how could I possibly do that? As I had been left in a standing position, I soon slid to the ground myself. Mother groaned loudly, then rolled over to help me. She propped me up once more. The two of us sat on the ground, breathing heavily, like two dogs that had been fighting. I looked at her but she didn't dare to look back. She beat the floor, shouting: 'Why do you want to be like this!'

'Mum, I love you!' I said.

'Nonsense.'

'Mum, do you love me?'

'Yes,' she said. 'But it is a different kind of love.'

'What is a different kind of love?' I said.

Mother said: 'I've wronged you. It was my fault that you became disabled. I can make it up to you. I can die for you!'

'If you can die, why can't you do something else?'

'That's impossible!'

'Why? Why, Mum?'

'That will hurt you,' she said.

She didn't say it was no good for her; just that she was afraid of hurting me. What an adorable mother!

'Can a mother hurt her child?'

She stared at me.

'Aren't you afraid of other people hurting me?'

'I promise to find you a good one!' she said. 'An excellent one! You believe your mum.'

'I believe you,' I said. 'But what do you mean by 'a good one'?'

'A virtuous one, a beauty,' my mother said. Her face lit up as she did her best to name all the qualities of an ideal wife. 'A one hundred per cent good wife, a perfect woman.'

'Mother, are you sure you are not describing a beautiful female snake?' I said. 'She will kill me.'

'She will make you very happy!' Mother said.

'She will suck me dry!' I said. 'Only Mum can nourish me.'

'No way!' Mother said. 'Anyway, you act like I'm not your mother.'

'Fine,' I said. 'If you are not my mother, then what's the problem?'

'So you take me to be a bad mother,' she said.

'If you are a bad mother, then why not do this?'

'I don't want to. That's good enough, isn't it?'

'Don't you have feelings for me, Mum?'

'I do not.'

'Really?'

'You mustn't force me,' Mother said.

'Don't bring disaster on me.'

Having said that, she went into a stupor and stared at me with empty, terrified eyes.

'Beat me to death, why not!' she suddenly said. 'I don't want to live! Beat me to death!'

She removed the cord from her nightclothes and put it in my hands. Then she used my hand to beat herself. What could I do? I resisted, but she was stronger than me. She gripped me so tightly it hurt. I cried out. She stopped, and painfully rubbed my hand. Suddenly she howled. 'I am not a good mum! You beat me! Beat me! Beat! Beat!'

3

'How about I use my hand?' Mother said later.

'No,' I said.

Now that I had pushed her so far, Mum seemed to have lost some of her shame. She still looked uncomfortable, though, standing before me.

'Do you think for a minute I am willing to accept that?' she said. 'Do you think that I am willing?'

She hurled a plate to the floor where it smashed into tiny pieces. That sound took the edge off the situation. It was as if we had argued over some trivial everyday problem.

She applied some lotion to me, and then she went and washed and dried her hands before returning. She reached out for me, then hesitated. Touching me there was already very natural to her. At bath times, she was the one who undressed me. Anyway, hadn't I come from her body? But now our lives were separate. When this came up, it was different.

Finally she used her index finger to poke me. Just as if it had been waiting for this, something popped out.

It felt very comfortable. Mother did it carefully. No pain. She simply tickled me, just like when I was little and had done something bad. Mother used one hand to tease me, almost hitting me as she rubbed. This was what a good mother could do. Her index finger stuck out; that red lotion was like blood.

The world outside was empty. There was only the two of us. Beyond our walls, there were sounds. There were street hawkers, there was a market. But they had nothing to do with me. I felt that the city was distant. I came. Her hand immediately pressed itself on the opening to stop more stuff from coming out as she cleaned up. Her reaction was so fast, it seemed as if she had already prepared. How did she know when I was going to cum? Maybe it was because she was my mum. She gave my penis a shake, to make my essence flow back. Then she wiped away the remainder from the tip, like a housewife scraping up every last remaining scrap of food or juice from a dish. Our

family never had any money. We always had to
save things, treasure them.

Afterwards, she went to wash her hands. I
saw her whole body. I caught sight of her bottom.
It was a little plump. The arse of a woman who has
had a child is very beautiful! I wanted it, and I
realized then that I wasn't satisfied. Using her hand
had been a kind of castration. No real hole had
been involved; in the analysis a hand was a
counterfeit hole.

'Mother, next time use your mouth,' I said.

'What?' Mother said. She looked at me like
I was a monster. 'No! How could you think of that?
You are more and more bad!'

'Yes, I am.'

'Where did you learn to be this bad?'
Mother said.

In fact, I had never even watched porn. I'd
just thought of it. If you have needs, then you think
about how to satisfy them. In this situation, people
don't need a teacher. I wasn't demanding to use
her oyster, just her mouth. At least it was a hole!

'Mother!' I said.

'Don't call me that,' she shouted. 'You have made me inhuman!'

'Just for a short time.'

'Not even for a short time! Aren't you making me into a cheap whore?'

'Love isn't cheap,' I said.

'Where did you learn to be so glib?' she said. 'I have already indulged you too much.'

I couldn't say anything to that. My lower body throbbed like it might explode. I started to moan. At first Mother ignored me, and then she went off and left me. I couldn't accompany her and so could only stay where I was. My body spasmed painfully. I thought about using my hand, but as soon as I touched myself I was repelled by a feeling of disgust. I shook despairingly and called out: 'Mother!'

Mother ignored me; I had never seen her so angry. I beat my meat and it felt like my penis had been yanked off. It was so painful that I cried out.

Mother finally returned. 'What are you doing?' she called out. 'Are you mad? That thing is the root of life. You'll kill yourself.'

'There's nothing I can do about it,' I cried.

'Then you will die!' Mother said.

'What is death to me? I don't care.'

'Listen, you are still talking nonsense,' Mum said. 'If you want to die, okay, but kill me first. Kill me first. Kill me!'

She seized my hand again, hit me, and then hit herself. She was still very strong and I couldn't resist. My hand was under her control. She lashed out and I lashed out. She beat, I beat. But I really did want to beat her because I was full of hate! Maybe I really did hate my mum. I beat her until we were both spent and she released my hand.

She suddenly said: 'Okay now.'

Okay? What was okay? Suddenly I realized that I no longer had a hard-on. I didn't know when it had subsided, but perhaps it was sublimation: the urgency of my desire displaced to the fury in my hand. My hand had become a substitute for my cock.

'Later, if you're suffering, then beat me again!' Mother said.

'No,' I said. 'I won't beat you.'

But I wanted to.

4

Use this!' Mother said. She'd got hold of a whip, a leather one. I don't know where from.

'I won't beat you!' I said.

'Mother tells you to beat her,' she said.

'No, I won't do it.'

'If I tell you to, you must beat!' she yelled.

Her shout gave me a violent start. I immediately took the whip from her hand.

'Just treat me like a bad mother!' she said.

'I won't do that!'

'Listen!' she said and pressed the whip into my hand. She closed my fingers around it and lashed it towards her body The whip swept a big wind across my face. It was a piercingly cold feeling, as if a big army was moving into place, a battle about to begin. To war! I heard Mother cry out.

'Painful?' I asked.

'Not painful, but painfully happy,' she answered. Her expression was strange.

These words, and her expression, stirred me, and the second lash came from me. The blow was lighter.

'That kind is painful,' she said.

'Why?'

'That kind of teasing blow is the worst,' she explained. 'The most agonizing.'

That was true. Sometimes when I hated myself, I would pinch my leg, and the most painful was when I did just a half pinch. I suddenly felt naughty, and whipped her lightly.

'Stupid child,' she said. 'Do you want Mother to have a difficult death?'

I laughed. 'Yes!' I said mischievously. 'I want you to suffer!'

She laughed too. 'Okay then. Who let me give birth to such a bad son!'

I knew that she was deliberately trying to present this situation as the normal matter of a bad son. That way we could do what we wanted.

Of course, Mother's pain was well-deserved, she said. I think she meant because she hadn't given me a healthy body. She was still making believe that our relationship was just a normal mother–son thing.

I said: 'No!'

'It is,' she said. 'Just think of it that way.'

5

'Mother, I want to make it wet.'

'Why?'

'Do it!' I said. I returned the whip to her.

Puzzled, she went to wet it. I saw the end of the whip drip water like it was blood. I brandished the whip and lashed. Mother gasped more sharply than before, just as I had expected. The wet whip was even more lethal but it didn't leave any mark.

'You, you are very bad! You are a bad egg!'

'Yes, I am! I want to be a real bad egg! In my life the only thing I really resented was that I couldn't be a really bad egg. I have finally become one. Your gift to me.'

Where had I got this vicious idea? No one had taught me. Maybe it was in my nature all along.

6

'Mum, I want to stand up and beat you,' I said.

'Okay,' Mother said.

She helped me to stand, and then lay down and supported me with her raised hand. I had a feeling of superiority. It was as if I was a normal person. I dominated the world, I had power. I lashed out.

But after a moment I couldn't stand any more because Mother's hand had released me. I was relying on her hand to stay propped up. When she felt pain, she couldn't help withdrawing her hand and I fell down. She lifted me again, as if she had just done something very wrong. In fact, all the best things she had done in her life had been for her son, and the worst thing had also been for her son: she had let her son fall down.

She supported me again. This way there was no way she could escape my lashes. We were enemies. I just wanted to make it clear that we were enemies!

7

'Mum, get up,' I said.

She lay there at the foot of the bed, a plane with no definite target to aim at. It was like hitting the bed, or the floor. There was no sense of violence.

'Mother, get up, give me something to aim at.'

7

Mum hugged me. Because she was so close to me,
I couldn't brandish my whip. But if she moved
away again, I couldn't stand up. I had no legs.
Bloody legs!

'Mother, let me stand on your back,' I said.

Mother lay on her stomach.

'Mum, get up,' I said.

8

Mum hugged me. Because we were so close
together, I couldn't brandish my whip. But if she
moved away again, I couldn't stand up. I had no
legs. My bloody legs!

'Mother, let me stand on your back,' I said.

Mother lay on her stomach.

9

My movements gradually became so clumsy that I couldn't hit accurately. I used too much force and dropped the whip. Mother crawled to get it.

'What's wrong with your hand?' she asked.

'Slightly hurt, it's nothing.'

'Who says!' Mother wrapped it up for me, and then examined the whip handle. 'Where was this made? So rough. Products these days are all poor quality.'

She decided to make a sheath for the handle; a cloth one, to protect my hand. She made it from rags she had collected. She chose one piece, but it wasn't wide enough, and so she found another and sewed them together. When she sewed them, you could hardly see the seam. I held it and it didn't rub against my hand. The cotton was soft, so soft it made me want to cry.

'It can't be too smooth or it won't stick to the handle; it will slide out. I need to get it just right.' She measured precisely, like this was a work of art. Afterwards, she admired her

handiwork. Maybe if the hand that beat her felt
pleasure, she felt pleasure too?

'Mother, are you really willing?' I asked.

'Mother is willing,' she said.

'Are you comfortable?' I said boldly.

'Comfortable,' she said.

'Nonsense, Mother,' I said. 'You are
always talking nonsense.'

'If you are comfortable, Mother is
comfortable.'

'But you don't look comfortable, Mother.
You just say you are because I am.'

'If you are comfortable, Mother is
comfortable, idiot!' Mother said. 'A child is part of
a mother's heart; if you are comfortable, of course
I am comfortable.'

'Mother, I don't want to be. I don't want to
be comfortable!'

'If you don't want to be comfortable,
Mother does!'

'Mother, I can make you comfortable,' I
said. 'I want to do that thing.' I pulled at her.

'Beat it!' Mother shouted. Never had she been so mad.

'You're driving me crazy, Mother!' I said. 'Are you angry with me?'

'No,' she said.

'No, I know you hate me! If you didn't have me, you would be better off.'

'Even if that was so,' Mother said, hardening herself to say it, 'don't you hate me? You shouldn't do, though. You have no future without me.'

'I do hate you!' I said.

'Okay then, hate me. If you hate me, you should beat me. Right? You cruel and unscrupulous person.'

'You cursed me well! I am unscrupulous.'

'Beat me!' Mother incited me.

So I beat her.

'Beat me again!'

So I beat her again. I hated my mum. I longed to do her in! She shouldn't have provoked me. All along she had deliberately provoked me.

She would rather have my hate than my love. She wanted to cultivate my hate, find satisfaction in it. She groaned; a very full-hearted groan. I groaned too. Another good groan. I brandished the whip. My whip was stiff!

'Very hard,' she cried out, and then instantly repressed herself. Maybe it wasn't from fear that the neighbours would hear; maybe she simply didn't want to waste her breath — like a jug of good wine holds in its vapours so that the bouquet can get more intoxicating. One blow at a time she became thoroughly intoxicated. She was so far gone that she didn't move. Mother, how can you only think of your own pleasure? What am I to do? You are selfish! But how can a mother not be selfish! Stop, I want you to wake up!

How could I make Ma wake up? Ah, I knew. I knew what she feared most! So I did it. As I did it I shouted: 'Ma, Ma! I love you, I love my mum! I love you, Mum.'

Clerk, make sure you got that down. Captain, don't gape. There's no need to stare. You feel sorry for me? You despise me? You say that my heart is dead? I will have to go on trial? I need to be paraded through the streets and exposed? My remains left out in the street? But there is one thing I would like to bring up in my defence! What? Animal sex. You have seen animals having sex? Well, we are animals. You don't admit it, I know. You say that doesn't apply to you, only me! You live dignified lives; wash away the placental blood and live in a civilized way; peaceful at heart.

Postscript

In 1877, Lewis H. Morgan in his work *Ancient Society* observed: 'American Iroquois Indians have a very unusual naming convention for kinsfolk. They don't only address their biological father as "Father", but also all of their father's brothers. For "Mother", it is the same. This form of address is like a living fossil which preserves information about primitive bloodlines.' Similarly in Chinese, the word 'jie' originally meant 'mother', as shown in a number of old works, and yet in common speech today the word is used to mean 'wife', 'lover' or 'young woman'. 'Niang' means 'mother', but the original meaning was 'young woman'. An ancient dictionary says: '*Niang*: a word meaning young girl'. The Southern Dynasties period poem 'Midnight Songs' has this lyric: 'See a young girl's happy enchanted face/hope to make a golden match'. But the word 'niangzi' also meant 'wife'.

The First Prohibition
By Chen Xiwo

At about the same time that I learned that this
English edition was planned, a verdict was reached
in my case relating to *I Love My Mum*. From the
start I had never believed that this work could be
passed by the China censors, and sure enough not
long after that the whole case that I had brought
against China's literary authorities was dropped.
The reason given was that this was the sixtieth
anniversary of the founding of New China.

The reason for my pessimism was because
of the fate of a collection of my work called *Book
of Offenses*. In 2007 an unabridged version of *Book
of Offenses* was published in Taiwan, but copies
sent to me in mainland China were seized, the most
important reason for this being that the book
contained *I Love My Mum*.

In 2004 on its publication in a southern literary magazine, this novella had been severely criticized. Beijing was notified and the Propaganda Ministry ordered its local office to take action. The executive editor of the magazine narrowly escaped the sack and had to submit to three weeks of criticism.

To be prohibited, to be criticized, is normal for me. Basically, everything I have published has either been banned or else extensively revised. Mainland China still has legions of censors willing to act as loyal guard dogs. Their paid work offers them two types of satisfaction: one is money, and the other is the feeling that they have convictions. They get money and they can have convictions: what could be better than that!

Of course, these censors are mainly hacks who don't really believe in what they are safeguarding. Just like everyone else, they love to read banned books, and they secretly curse the government even more than other people. As soon as they put on their censor's cap though, they are again the embodiment of the government, operating with the authority of the state.

Nowhere is it explicitly stated what is not permitted; the whole system depends on 'self-censorship'. The editor of one literary journal once told me that he himself didn't know what he could or couldn't publish. As a result, most people operate within ever tighter restraints. They say it is "the people" restraining you, but "the people" never asked the government to stop them reading what they wanted.

In 2005, my novel *Scratching an Itch* was banned as soon as it appeared. Simultaneously, the same publishing house's *Serve the People* by Yan Lianke was also banned. *Scratching an Itch* was banned because of sexual content, and *Serve the People* because of politics. The publishing house and its editors came under great pressure. At the time there were those who said that because *Serve the People*'s problem was politics, there was still hope in that case, because political lines are always

subject to reversal, but *Scratching an Itch*'s
problem was sex and so it could never be redeemed.

All through the ages, sex has been the first
prohibition. But why does sex need this rigorous
supervision? In any society, ordinary people, if
they are intent on sex, won't pay any attention to
government, while rulers are even more likely to
do as they please. But sex is political. Any regime
will always put the Marquis de Sade in jail.

Of course, I am writing about public sex.
Sex, if you can only keep it in the shadows, can
still flourish. In today's China, many places rely on
sex to drive their economic growth. These are
known as 'prostitute economies'. Those raised in a
culture of shame don't believe in the omnipresence
of God, only in the scrutiny of others. Twenty
years ago, if people wanted to join the Communist
Party, others would shun them; today things have
changed.

In this world I don't look for moral virtue,
because there is none and there never has been.

What moral codes mainly prove is that past generations have never lived up to them.

Of course the existence of these codes represents a challenge to evil. Even if people behave in a despicable way, there can be moments of illumination; even if they don't change their behaviour, they may realize what they are doing. If this is all, it is already no small thing; the beginnings of human awareness. In *I Love My Mum* the central character has just this kind of awakening. In this respect he is not only no degenerate, he is even a model for morality in our generation. When he realizes that the object of his desire is his own mother, he shouts it out, wakes his mother up, lifts the covers, acknowledges his crime.

This is my style of writing, although lots of people don't understand why I want to write this way. It causes them embarrassment. It makes people unhappy, makes them anxious. People look at me like I am an evil spirit. Well I prefer to be this kind of evil spirit, rather than an angel who sings all day long in praise of "virtue", or of some 'golden age of China."

A country whose GDP has reached middle-income country level apparently still feels the need to sacrifice people to economics. Well a country without people at its core is worthless; a writer with no dignity, writing what he is told, accepting of being banned and censored, is a coward, and this writer will only write rubbish.

I am not willing to write rubbish, and I am not willing to be a coward

Chen Xiwo: Rebel

In June 2007, the Fuzhou office of China Customs intercepted a package addressed to a teacher of Japanese literature at a local university. The customs officers ascertained that the package contained twelve copies of a book that had been mailed by a Taiwanese publisher to the academic, who was in fact its author. The book, a collection of short novels, was quickly deemed 'prohibited' because it contained the 'pornographic' and 'anti-human' novella *I Love My Mum*.

What happened next was perhaps unprecedented in the history of the People's Republic of China. The author, Chen Xiwo, launched a legal case against China Customs for confiscating his book. For centuries, Chinese writers had more or less accepted the right of the authorities to act as censors of their work. If a work was banned then writers would typically agree to make a self-criticism. But Chen Xiwo went to court, and an uproar exploded in the Chinese media at the absurdity of a writer having his own book confiscated.

The scandal surrounding Chen Xiwo's novel *I Love My Mum* in many ways epitomizes a writing career characterized by a refusal to compromise. Chen Xiwo is a child of the Cultural Revolution, and his work preserves the flavour of that Zeitgeist: the demand for an impossible 'purity', coupled with first-hand knowledge of the amoral darkness at the heart of human nature. Above all, an appetite for unrelenting struggle. For many years Chen went unpublished. Even when, in the early 2000s, he began to win recognition and prizes, his work continued to divide opinion due to its pessimistic view of human nature and its preoccupation with dark sexuality.

In 2007, Chen's collection of novellas, *Book of Offenses* (冒犯书), was published by China's prestigious People's Literature Publishing House (Renmin Wenxue Chubanshe). For some, this collection represents the pinnacle of Chen's

writing career to date. Like the Polish director
Krzysztof Kieslowski's *Decalogue* film series,
each story was supposedly inspired by one of the
Ten Commandments. However, one story was
missing from the collection as published in China –
deemed beyond the pale even for a collection of
such literary merit: *I Love My Mum*.

Even those who are not generally inclined
to side with China's censors may feel some
empathy in this case. *I Love My Mum* concerns one
of the deepest human taboos, incest – and it
doesn't pull its punches. Because of its status as a
cause célèbre and the extreme reactions it provokes,
I Love My Mum has in many ways become the
work by which Chen's writing is judged.

Chen Xiwo is from Fujian province, which
he credits with having helped to shape his values.
Fujian, in southeast China, adjacent to Taiwan, has
historically been on the margins of the Chinese
empire, usually receiving attention from emperors
only in times of crisis. Fujian was also one of the
first parts of China to feel the influence of western

cultures, both in the late Qing dynasty, when the area enjoyed a commercial flourishing, and in the 1980s after Deng launched his opening-up policy and it became the host of one of China's special economic zones. Yet in the first half of the twentieth century, on the 'frontline' of many of the conflicts that consumed China in those decades, Fujian became poor. These currents combined to give the province the flavour of a region apart, and may have helped contribute to what Chen describes as his 'distance' from the Chinese mainstream.

In the 1980s, Chen Xiwo got the chance to go to college where he studied with 'Misty Poetry' school poet Sun Shao Zhen (孙绍振.) Unsurprisingly, Chen was a radical student, to the forefront of the debate and ferment that developed in a more liberal intellectual climate in the middle of the decade. His parents grew concerned that he would get into trouble and decided to send him to study abroad. With prescient timing, he left for Australia in 1989, just a few months before the Tiananmen uprising. The events of 4 June confirmed Chen's belief that it was better for the moment for him to develop his career outside of China. He soon moved to Tokyo where he embarked on a PhD in comparative literature, and altogether Chen was to remain away from China for seven years.

It wasn't only developments in China that kept him away for so long, however; he had embarked on a love affair with Japan and Japanese literature. It was during this period in Japan that many of Chen's important preoccupations as a writer took shape. Out of sympathy with prevailing currents in Chinese literature, he admired Japanese writers' characteristic concern with individual psychology rather than social responsibility, with weirdness rather than conformity. His affinity for the dark concision of writers like Yukio Mishima and Junichiro Tanizaki is evident in his own work.

Chen's stay in Japan also allowed him to further develop his interest in the theme of 'perverse' sexuality — although he disavows the term, as he regards all sexuality as 'perverse'. To

fund his studies Chen worked for a time as a
Tokyo mama-san, which may have influenced the
topic of his ultimately unfinished comparative
literature doctoral thesis: S&M. Chen's view that
'sex is always the first prohibition of power' owes
a lot to his reading of both the Marquis de Sade
and French philosopher Michel Foucault's *History
of Sexuality*.

In Chen's view, Japanese literature was far
superior to Chinese in its treatment of sex. Chinese
writers wrote about sex in a superficial way, or else
treated it purely as fun. Rarely did even the
Chinese classics, like *Jin Ping Mei (*金瓶梅), focus
on the dark side of human sexuality. Chen's works
explore the link between dysfunctional society and
dysfunctional sexuality, arguing that 'extreme'
sexual behaviour is often the sign of a soul and a
culture in a poor state of health. This terrain is one
Chen returns to again and again.

Chen eventually returned to his native
Fujian province and took up a comparative
literature teaching position at a university there. In

the early years of the twenty-first century his work finally reached a wider audience through the internet. Chen's talent was gradually recognized; and in 2001 he won his first major award, the Chinese Literature Media Prize (华语文学传媒大奖), with *My Dissipation* (我们的苟且). This brought him to the attention of the literati, and his works won further awards.

Nevertheless, Chen's relationship with the literary authorities remained difficult. It was impossible for his work to be published without being cut or banned, which engendered considerable misunderstanding of his writing in China, where he was sometimes viewed mainly as a pornographer even by (especially by) his fans.

ii

I Love My Mum is often held up as proof of Chen's anti-humanism. In fact, despite his interest in Foucault's ideas, Chen draws back from Foucault's contention that 'human nature' is a bourgeois construct. On the contrary, as the

structure of *Book of Offenses*, with its framework
based loosely on the Ten Commandments, suggests,
Chen has traditional moral concerns. The novella
does not merely advance a generalized bleak view
of human nature, but a view of China specifically
as a society ruined by its lack of freedoms and
failure to place 'people' at its centre.

Chen deliberately sets *I Love My Mum* in a
city that has been corrupted by the lust for wealth.
The opening paragraph establishes the context after
the police captain has been too zealous in his
'cleaning-up' operation. His superior reprimands
him, saying: *'The sex industry is a pillar of our
city's economy. Do you want us to get rich? Well,
a city has to rely on whatever resources it has.
What we have here is prostitutes.'*

The murderer's 'amoral' reasoning, far
from being aberrant, echoes:that of the police chief.

*'Morality?' He laughed coldly. 'Morality
is for those who have enough ...'*

Chen's China is a society where rank
crimes such as the Tiananmen killings and the

Cultural Revolution have gone unacknowledged, leaving a corrupting stench. When the neighbours in the story visit the house and the mother blocks the doorway, they comment that *a sour smell seeped out from behind her body.*

In Chen's analysis, it is natural that political crimes should find their parallel in the sexual realm. For Chen, China is held back by a pathological inability to acknowledge wrongdoing. As the police captain reflects: ... *how often do we think about our souls? We continue on our individual paths to destruction.* At the very start of the story, Chen makes it clear that the captain's job is as much to cover up crimes as to uncover them: we first encounter him not arresting suspects but letting them go. Later, the murderer senses that the authorities do not really want to confront his crime of killing his mother. They are ready to downplay what he has done, to find excuses rather than confront the horrors of our human nature.

In Chinese society, Chen argues, there is no interest in truth; only in 'business as usual'. Indeed,

Chen shows that language itself is primed to deflect and conceal reality: the phrase 'talking nonsense' is used by all three main characters to deflect unpleasant realities. In Chen's view, one symptom of this lack of moral awareness is failure to confront one's true sexual desires, as when the police captain refuses to admit that he masturbates:

I had done often, of course ... But to his face I lied. I am a cop, I couldn't admit to that.

Despite appearances then, *I Love My Mum* is very much a political novel. For Chen, in a China groaning with hidden corruption, the 'morality' of the narrator lies precisely in his eventual willingness to admit to his foul deeds, to shout them out. In Chen's view, this kind of honesty is the best that can be hoped for in China at this time, and marks the beginning of a 'human awareness'. Chen thus draws back from Foucault's contention that 'human nature' is a bourgeois construct, and remains invested in a concept of the human which, however problematic epistemologically, remains the foundation of resistance to power.

Chen's refusal to compromise has bound him in a lifelong love–hate relationship with the Chinese authorities. One suspects that Chen obtains a measure of satisfaction from it, and he once wrote the following: 'In this sort of country where there is no hope, to continue to seek the courage to keep living is precisely to embrace an S&M relationship where one finds pleasure in being abused'. Yet this tension continues to fuel the creativity of an important voice of conscience in contemporary China. Chen Xiwo's powerful works are an urgent, courageous cry for China to confront its social and political ills, and for his readers to acknowledge their most subversive desires.

I Love My Mum

Translators' Acknowledgements

This translation would not have been possible without the contribution of several people. Special thanks must go to Nicola O'Shea for her thoughtful editorial work, to Claire Li and Jasmine Ye for their helpful suggestions, and to Nick Berriff for Japanese lessons. Thanks also to Hao Qun, to whom this translation is dedicated for his support. Finally I must express my gratitude to Chen Xiwo for his enthusiasm for this project and refusal to compromise.

Chen Xiwo

Modern Chinese Masters

<u>Forthcoming Titles</u>

Working Girls

by Sheng Keyi.

Translation by Han Jing

December 2009

Hong thought, I've committed adultery, I've had affairs and I've done things to please myself, but none of that was for money.

Working Girls is the defiant, humorous, and moving story of two young Hunan girls who leave home with dreams of starting a new life in Shenzhen. The novel was a sensation after it was published in China and turned writer Sheng Keyi into a literary superstar. *Working Girls* follows the girls' adventures as they move between short-lived factory and hotel jobs, overcoming numerous challenges

Make-Do Publishing

I Love My Mum